Angel Dancer

by

Frances Mary Hendry

Illustrated by Shelagh McNicholas

First published in 2004 in Great Britain by
Barrington Stoke Ltd, Sandeman House, Trunk's Close,
55 High Street, Edinburgh EH1 1SR

ISBN 1-842991-84-1

Printed by Polestar Wheatons Ltd

A Note from the Author – Frances Mary Hendry

As an English teacher for over 20 years I learned the bits of books that my pupils dodged reading, and I try not to write like that. I won a competition to have my first book published. The competition was called "Quest for a Kelpie", but by mistake that's what I called my entry and it won. Whoopee!

I produce pantos, and act, usually as a witch or a dragon. I'm a bookaholic. At the moment I have five books on the go, one each in the bedroom, bathroom, living-room, kitchen and the room where I write. I cook with a spoon in one hand and a book in the other – it's only a matter of time before I stir the stew with the book. Books are magic!

To Mum, who took me to
ballet lessons at Miss
Hopkins' school so many
years ago, and always
bought me a cream bun
afterwards

Contents

Chapter 1
Ballet

I'm over 60 now, but I can still do a perfect ballet sixth position with the edges of my feet touching. I can kick my foot as high as my head and I can lay my hands flat on the floor between my feet without bending my knees. Ballet training does that for you, even the three years I did, an hour every Saturday morning so long ago.

I could never really have been a dancer. I'm long in the back and short in the legs, just the wrong way round. And I've always been big. To be a dancer I'd have had to slim down till I dropped, and I enjoyed food too much. I liked the dancing, but in the end I decided that it wasn't worth the pain and strain to go on. I'd got as much as I could out of the lessons. I could stand tall and move lightly and gracefully, and I could dance in time to music – moving my feet, too, the way youngsters don't these days. They just stand and wave their arms about, and think that's dancing. Huh!

Anyway, I stopped dancing lessons when I was about 12, but my sister Brenda carried on. She was two years older than me, but smaller and lighter, like a fairy, an elf. She looked like a sweet little angel, but she was the wildest wee tearaway in Maryhill, perhaps in the whole of Glasgow, and that was saying something.

She wasn't bad at home, mind. Mum didn't stand for any nonsense. If we argued or were cheeky, she smacked us good and hard – she didn't wait for Dad to come home. She couldn't – Dad was away in the Navy! Mum saw to it that we were fairly polite to each other, as well as to everybody else, at least when she could see us.

Beyond that, well, I was always a quiet wee soul, too shy to make trouble, but Brenda was a real fighter.

Maryhill in Glasgow was a real mixed area in those days, before it was all rebuilt and cleaned up. There were some nice blocks of flats but lots were horrible. Some were very tough, even the wally ones – the ones with tiled walls in the stairwells – we called those closes. They were much posher than the ones with painted walls, with shared toilets and broken banisters. We lived in a wally close.

I stayed near Mum when we were out.
I loved reading and didn't go out to play
much. I had stabbing pains in my legs,
growing pains, Mum said, and she kept me
in while Brenda was away out with her
friends playing all round the streets and in
the Botanic Gardens. They used to paddle in
the stinking, brown River Kelvin, climb the
high walls with sharp bits of glass on the
top and shout rudely at the soldiers in
Maryhill Barracks till the guards chased
them away. If there was nothing better to
do they used to play down among the
washing-line poles and rubbish bins behind
the closes, in the back green. I never got
into any trouble. I kept well clear of it.

One day, though, I had to start school.

Chapter 2
School

I can't remember why Mum didn't take me to school that first day. It's so long ago. Brenda rushed me along the road. She was keen to meet her own friends after the summer holidays. She pulled me through the gate and showed me the stinking shed with the toilets.

"That's the girls' bogs. The doors are all broken and the chains are bust so they don't flush. They never mend them 'cos they just get broken again, so hold on if you can but if you've got to go you just hold your nose and get in and out quick as you can. But don't go in the boys' ones round the other side, they're worse!"

How did she know?

She left me standing in a corner, watching the other children jumping, running and shouting all round the yard. When the bell went she remembered me. She shoved me into the infants' classroom, told the teacher my name, and darted off to her own class.

Mum had told me to be good, sit still and be polite to the teachers, so I did.

That wasn't the proper way to behave, not in Maryhill in those days.

A few of the toughest pupils got annoyed at me. When we put on our coats and were sent out at break, at eleven, they all crowded round me in the playground.

I was plump, I wore glasses, I was tidy and dressed neatly in a clean, ironed skirt and blouse. They were dirty, rough lads and girls in torn skirts or shorts and jumpers full of holes. Their matted hair was wild, their noses, red-raw. Their socks – if they had any – didn't match and wrinkled round their grey ankles above tatty sandshoes or big, clumpy tackety boots passed down from older brothers and sisters. A few of them even had bare feet. Some had been kept back a year, or even two, so they were bigger than me. Some of their big brothers and sisters came over to see what was happening and join in the fun. They sneered at me, shoving me about and calling me names.

"Teacher's pet! Look at Lady Muck! Swot! Fat wee piggy, thinks she's clever! We'll show you!"

They loomed over me, poking me, slapping, shoving, pinching, spitting on me, tugging the ribbons off my tidy hair, throwing my glasses away across the playground.

I tried not to cry, but I was terrified. I had never, ever met children like this before. I couldn't get away. There were tall railings with spikes on all round the playground, and the gate was locked. No teachers came into the yard at break, not in those days. You were expected to look after yourself – even if you couldn't. Like me.

"Come on, shove her in the bin! Nah, down the bog-hole! Head first!"

I couldn't move for terror.

Then Brenda came yelling in on them. There were about eight of them, and Brenda was smaller even than me, but she chased them! "Clear out o' here, you rotten bullies! You leave my wee sister alone or I'll gut you!"

Fierce as a weasel she was, and she'd do anything. Anything at all. They knew her. She'd have stuck a finger in their eye and ripped it out, just as soon as slap them, any of them.

"It's that crazy Brenda! Come on! Run!" and they fled.

"And don't you try that again! If I see youse botherin' her again I'll melt youse!" she screeched after them, while I clung to her with deep relief. She shoved me off fast. She didn't like softies. "Don't be daft, you!"

When I was standing alone, she sniffed at me and laughed. "You're soft, Mary. Soppy! You've got to stand up for yourself or they'll walk all over you. And I'll not be here all the time. Just you remember, you'll get hurt worse if you're scared than if they are, so go for it! Whatever it costs, you've got to go for it! That's the only way to win."

Even I was a bit scared of her, though I loved her. She kept an eye on me, in a casual kind of way that still protected me from the worst in the playground. I was grateful.

She always went out with me on Sunday mornings to Sunday School but skived off to play while I went along to the church like a good little girl. She laughed herself silly when I told her I prayed for her. "You think that'll do any good? Don't bother God and he'll no bother you, that's what I say!" I was shocked.

Chapter 3
The Angel

Brenda started dancing after I did. Mum asked me what I wanted for Christmas when I was eight, and I said ballet lessons. Brenda laughed herself silly all over again. "Who d'you think you are, Princess Elizabeth?" But Mum agreed.

Next Saturday morning we went on two trams to Charing Cross in town, up some stairs and across an open space. We had arrived.

"Look, Mum," I said, "on that wall, there's a big, gold angel holding a lily! Is this a church?"

It was really just a statue looking out over the street, put there to look posh when the house was built a hundred years ago. But I didn't know that then, and the angel comforted me. I felt quite scared, and it was good to know that there was someone watching over me.

Mum shrugged. "Maybe it's a war memorial. I don't know. Come along, here's the door. See the brass plate?"

"Hopkins Academy of Music and Dance," I read out. "Music? Academy? I just want ballet lessons."

She laughed. "An academy is just a posh name for a school, pet. It means you'll learn the best kind of dancing here. Now come on, we'll be late."

I started out in the baby class, the Seventh Grade. It was the last one of the morning. There were about 40 of us in the class, and old Miss Hopkins was strict. She hit us with her walking stick if we misbehaved or chattered. She insisted we must pay attention, turn out our toes and keep our bottoms tucked in.

Each week, we arrived at 12.20, in time to hang up our coats and change into ballet shoes – just little slip-on ones to begin with, or bare feet. Mum wouldn't have let anybody think we couldn't afford dancing shoes. So at first, till she knew if I'd carry on, she sewed me a couple of pairs from an old heavy satin petticoat of Gran's, with soles cut out of an old, pink handbag. When the next class up came out of their lesson at 12.30, we trooped into the big room and lined up to curtsey to Miss Hopkins.

I loved that room. The old wind-up gramophone stood on the piano in one corner and played our music for us most of the time. For special occasions a lady came to play the piano.

You could watch yourself in a huge mirror along one wall. I felt a bit embarrassed. Mum always said looking at yourself in mirrors made you big-headed and you'd come to a bad end. I used to wonder what a bad end was! But the angel outside would look after me, I hoped.

Half a crown a week it cost, two shillings and sixpence, that's twelve pence now, for half an hour's lesson. That was more than an hour's wage for a workman, at least ten pounds these days, I suppose. I did babysitting three evenings a week, for the woman next door who was a barmaid in a pub, to help pay for my lessons. This was long before the rules that stopped children working before and after school. We thought that was only common sense. When you only got pennies, or nothing, from your parents, a bob or two of your own felt wonderful.

Anyway, I'd been doing ballet for a year. I'd taken the first exams and moved up to the Sixth Grade class. They went in at 12 o'clock – and it cost three shillings a lesson. That Christmas Mum took Brenda and me both to the King's Theatre for our treat. We went to see Alicia Markova dance in *Swan Lake*. I cried, it was so beautiful. I still do, when I think back.

Brenda never moved all the way through. When we came out she turned to Mum and said, "That's what I'm going to do. I'm going to be a dancer. A great dancer. Like Markova."

Mum was a bit taken aback – well, it's not what most wee girls from Glasgow back streets want to do. However, after some argument, she agreed. "If you'll help pay for it, Brenda, like Mary does, you can have lessons too."

Brenda just nodded. "I'll do a paper round."

Mum was surprised again because it was usually boys who did paper rounds. But it paid better than babysitting.

Brenda had a double round by the next week. She had to be up and out by 5.30 every morning, even Sundays, and she never missed one, even in snow or blinding rain and sleet. She put a shilling towards her lesson every week.

Then Dad left the Navy and came home. He soon got a job as chief of security in a

big firm and his pay just about doubled.
And Mum got a part-time job in a shop.
So we got a bit of pocket money. I stopped
the babysitting. Brenda could have stopped
the paper round, but she didn't.

Chapter 4
An Extra-special Pupil

When Brenda started ballet lessons, I wondered how she'd get on. Old Miss Hopkins used to walk round among us with her stick. If our bottoms or our knees stuck out, she'd hit them to make us tuck them in again. I thought that Brenda would fly out at her, the same as she did at the teachers. When she passed the 11-plus exam and got into the High School, she still got belted and told off all the time for being cheeky and swearing. But she stayed calm for Miss Hopkins.

She joined the grade below me and she worked so hard that in three months she was moved up to my class, and then into the grade above, and then up again, without bothering about exams. We went to the ballet school together, to save Mum having to take us. I didn't like that when Brenda moved up, because I had to go in time for *her* class which was before mine. I had to sit and wait. But Miss Hopkins let me bring a book and sit on the piano stool to read, as long as I worked the gramophone for her. A special favour, for Brenda's sister.

Because Brenda was special.

The rest of us did our best, but we clumped about and the boards creaked under us. When Brenda danced, there was silence except for the softest twittering of her ballet shoes on the floor. She moved as if the music on the scratchy, old records was pulling her along, as if she was floating on the air. She had perfect balance and perfect timing, and she knew, every moment, exactly what her body, arms and legs, head, hands and feet were doing – and that kind of control is something you can't be taught. You either have it or you don't.

In the ballet class, her face was like a mask. She never smiled, or looked excited. She never whispered on the benches at the side, the way we did, while someone else was dancing. She watched, concentrating, eating up every movement, every word, learning what to do – and what not to do – as if her life depended on it. She always, always, always did every exercise as beautifully as she could. Everything, from walking into the room to grand spins and poses, whatever she did was done perfectly. She never preened at the mirrors, as we did. You could see that when she watched herself in the mirror, she wasn't admiring herself. She was checking that her dancing was flawless.

After class she'd change back into her outdoor clothes and shoes in silence.
It would take her ten minutes to return to normal again.

Nobody made any fuss about it. It was just the way Brenda was.

The rest of us just tried to ignore her. She was a bit embarrassing.

At home, she and I shared a bedroom and a double bed, which took up most of the space. Brenda shoved the bed back against the wall to leave some space where she could practise on the blue lino floor every night after doing her homework. She practised for hours and hours, until after ten some nights. The woman in the flat below knocked on her ceiling, and then came up to complain about the noise. Mum was furious at Brenda for causing trouble. Brenda didn't stop, though. She just started dancing in her bare feet. Her toes grew so strong she could do point work and dance on her toes without blocked shoes. She took an old rug out of somebody's dustbin to muffle the noise, and practised before doing her homework instead of after. Sometimes she was too tired to do her homework at all, and got belted again, but she never cared. "It doesn't matter, Mary!" she'd say. "It's worth it! It's worth anything!"

Not to me it wasn't. I slept beside the wall, so that Brenda could get up first for her paper round. That meant if I had to get up at night to go to the bathroom, I woke her, and I hated that. I knew she needed her sleep.

The dancing did something to Brenda. It changed her. She was calmer, withdrawn, as if she was listening to music all the time inside her head and had no time for anything else. She even stopped fighting at school. When anybody annoyed her, she'd just grin and turn away as if they were silly kids. That really peeved people. They called her all sorts of names – snooty, snotty madam was the least of it! But when a girl actually attacked her one day, Brenda burst into a fighting rage just like her old self, so they stopped.

After two years, Brenda was already working with the First and Second Grade class that went in at nine. I was still in Fifth Grade, but I was old enough now to go by myself, which was a relief.

Miss Hopkins asked if Brenda would like to join the very first class that she held at eight on Saturday mornings, for her extra-special pupils. Brenda agreed. She didn't even ask Mum and Dad. She told us all at tea that night.

They sat with the sausage and eggs getting cold on their plates, and stared at her. "Extra lessons?" Mum said in astonishment. "Just who do you think you are, madam? Where do we find the money, I'd like to know? We need every penny—"

"Now, Mum," Dad said, and Mum shut up. He never said much, did Dad, but when he did we all listened. Now he just looked at Brenda. "Is it really important to you, Brenda?"

She nodded. "Yes, Dad. More than anything."

"Right." He looked at Mum. "How much will it cost?"

"The ordinary class is four pounds a term now for each of them. That's bad enough. Then there's a new pair of blocked ballet shoes at ten shillings every year, even if I darn them." Mum shrugged. "And how much does this special class cost?"

"It's twice as much, Mum. And I'd need to go on with the ordinary class, too," Brenda said. Mum gasped in shock.

"But I've got money." Brenda was dead serious. "I've never given up my paper rounds, and I haven't spent a penny. Half a crown a week, all my birthday and Christmas present money, too. I've got 23 pounds. That can all go towards it."

For once, Mum was silenced. Twenty-three pounds was a terrific amount for a girl of 13 to save in those days.

Dad nodded. "I can see you take it serious, lassie," he said.

"I'll stop my ballet, Dad – then Brenda can have my lesson money," I said. I wanted a good excuse to stop. I'd never be as good as Brenda, anyway. Brenda looked at me with amazement. I shrugged. "Next year I'm going into Fourth Grade. They do point work, dancing on their toes. I've watched them coming out of their class and they unwind cotton wool from round their toes. It's covered in blood and they're often crying because it hurts so bad. No way is ballet worth that! I'm too big. I'll never be a ballerina. So why go on?"

"It *is* worth it!" Brenda muttered. "But thanks."

"Well," Dad rubbed his chin, "I think, Brenda, if you keep up your paper rounds and put that money in, we'll make up the rest. It depends on you. It'll be a strain for us to pay the extra, even with Mary giving up her class. So you'll have to show willing, too. If you drop your paper rounds, you can use up your savings if you want to for lessons. But when you stop putting in your money every week, we'll stop paying the rest. Is that fair?"

For the first time since we'd left the ballet class that day, Brenda smiled. It was like a rainbow. It lifted your heart.

The next week, when I went for my last lesson, I looked up at the angel for the last time. "Thanks for looking after me and getting me out of this stupid ballet!" I told her, inside my head. "Now you don't have two of us to see to, you can concentrate on looking after Brenda. Do a good job!"

From then on, Brenda worked even harder. Her paper rounds took more than two hours before school every day. As well as the time she spent practising at home, Miss Hopkins let her go into the studio right after school, to work in front of the mirror wall there for an hour before the evening classes started, and for hours on Sundays, without charging her.

We all knew that Brenda was heading for something great, one of the big ballet companies – maybe even Sadler's Wells in London!

Chapter 5
Another Markova?

Every Christmas, Miss Hopkins produced a show with her pupils. Everybody came, not just parents, because she polished up her best pupils to a really high standard. Miss Hopkins had a great sense of style – her shows were worth watching. All her ex-pupils came, with their children, and a lot of outsiders came as well, just for the show. Brenda always had a good part, even when she was in the baby classes.

In the next show, they did a bit out of *Swan Lake*.

For this, Brenda needed a white satin tutu with a stiff net skirt. We couldn't afford to buy one, so Mum made it out of an old wedding dress she bought from a friend. Because she didn't have a sewing machine she sewed all the stiff net layers onto the heavy satin by hand until her fingers bled. She said it was worth it, to see Brenda looking a treat. Mum bought white tights and new shoes, though, pink ones, with blocked toes, of course, and wide satin ribbons.

Although Brenda was still only 14, she was going to dance a big solo, alone on stage. It wasn't snappy and showy, all fast flicking spins and dazzle. That only needs confidence and oomph to get over any mistakes and make everyone clap. No, Brenda's solo was much more difficult.

It was slow and stately to show off her rock-steady balance and drifting, elegant style. She practised it every night at home, humming the music to herself till I was sick of it. However, it was worth it. On the night she did it beautifully, and got one of the biggest rounds of applause that evening.

The next day, it was Brenda who had her picture in the papers, not the older girls. "Another Markova?" and "Prima Ballerina in the Making!" the headlines said. Mum was so proud of her, she cut out the article and photo. "I'll start a scrap-book!"

Brenda herself just shrugged. "Markova? Huh! Stupid gits!" she said. "Don't know what they're talking about! But I'll do it yet!" She winked at me. "Your angel's doing her stuff, eh?" She held the new shoes close to her heart, and put them away on her shelf carefully as if they were made of gold. She'd not use them for ordinary classes.

Brenda and I shared the same bed, as we'd always done, but we didn't see much of each other those days. She was out in the morning before I woke up. She went to school straight after her paper rounds. Most days she went off to ballet right after school, running the mile to Miss Hopkins' studio. She wouldn't take the tram, of course – it would cost money, and every penny went to pay for lessons.

Then in February Miss Hopkins told us that the King's Theatre was putting on a Charity Show, and the Hopkins Academy had been asked to repeat the *Swan Lake* dances. She was quite excited about it.

So was Brenda. "Miss Hopkins says a teacher from Sadler's Wells will be there!" she told us, her face flushed with excitement. "She'll speak to him about me, and if he likes me, they'll test me for a place! She thinks I could even get a

scholarship to pay all the fees, boarding and everything!"

Dad looked worried. "You'd have to go down to London so they can try you out?" London was a very long way away and not the place for young girls on their own.

"Don't worry, Dad, I'll go with her!" said Mum. By now, she was as fired up as Brenda was. "We'll stay with your cousin in Watford. I'll need to get a new hat and gloves!"

Brenda grinned at her. "You'll need them for the theatre here anyway, Mum. Princess Margaret's going to be there for our Charity Show, in the King's! It'll be a royal performance!"

"Oh, that's wonderful!"

Mum loved the royal family.

But the Sadler's Wells man was worth more to Brenda. I sent grateful thoughts to the angel – just as a joke.

I think it was that same night that Brenda started crying in the bed, huddled as far away from me as she could get under the blankets, so that she'd not disturb me.

"What is it?" I grunted sleepily, and then woke up properly. I'd never seen Brenda cry before. Not ever.

"Nothing!" she muttered, and wouldn't tell me.

Even if I was three inches taller than her by then, I was still just her young sister, and we'd grown apart over the last year. I couldn't cuddle her, and say, "Come on, now, tell me what's wrong!" I thought maybe she was worried about the show. But if I woke up in the night, I could never get back to sleep properly. So when Brenda got up in the dark before dawn, I woke too. I saw how carefully and slowly she pulled on her right sock and shoe. She stood up, put her weight on that foot, pushed gently up onto her toes – and her breath hissed sharply in through her teeth as she dropped back onto her left foot.

"Brenda?" I muttered.

She jumped. "Are you awake?"

"That's a right daft question! No, I'm still asleep! What is it?"

"Never mind. Go back to sleep, Mary!"

"What's wrong with your foot?" I asked.

"Nothing!" she snapped. Then she huffed, and said, "I just twisted my ankle yesterday. It's nothing. It'll be OK tomorrow." She walked out, not limping.

Over the next month, Brenda got very thin, and she was small to start with. Mum started to worry about her, but Brenda just laughed. "Don't worry, Mum! It's excitement! You can't say I'm not eating well!" True enough, she was wolfing her meals. She didn't look pale or act ill.

She had so much self-control that nobody else noticed that her ankle was still bad. It hurt if she turned too fast on it, and it was a bit swollen, too. She never limped, or showed it hurt. No one could see anything was wrong unless they were looking for it. I was. I was worried. That twisted ankle didn't seem to be mending.

"Come on, angel!" I prayed. "Help her. If she has to give up this show she'll be heartbroken – and after all her hard work and dedication it really wouldn't be fair."

Then one day, a week before the show, I saw Brenda coming out of the bank.
"Hi, Brenda!" I called.

She jumped a foot and flushed blotchy scarlet. "What do you want?" she demanded angrily.

I was taken aback. "Nothing!" I protested. "I just said 'Hi'. What's all the fuss about? What were you doing in the bank?"

"None o' your business!" she snarled at me, and turned away – but in her fluster she didn't pay attention. She jerked her right foot and gave a gasp of pain.

"Your ankle's still bothering you," I said. I was worried. "It's really bad, isn't it? Maybe you should see the doctor—"

"I'm not giving up the show!" She hissed it at me, just one hot, red patch on each cheek standing out like tulips against the sheet-white of her face. "Never! I'm all right! I'll be all right!"

I shook my head. "I was only going to say why don't you give up your paper round!" I snapped back at her. And then I knew. She already had. She was getting money out of the bank to give to Mum. Without telling anybody.

Brenda saw that I guessed. "Keep your nose out of it!" she yelled at me in a strangled scream. "It's none o' your business! I'm going to dance – I am! I've got to! It's my chance – my chance to get noticed, to get into a proper ballet school. I can't not! My ankle's a bit sore, that's all! It's worth it! I'll get it seen to afterwards. So you keep your big, flappy mouth shut, you hear me? If you tell Mum or Dad, I'll kill you!"

In the playground people were always yelling, "I'll murder you!" in the heat of the moment. Brenda did it too. But this time – this time I had the feeling that she meant it.

I didn't know what to do. I should tell Mum if there really was something wrong. But I could have made a mistake. And Brenda was older than me. And fierce. She scared me when she was so fierce. So if it was that important to her ... well ...

In the end, I did nothing. In my head I prayed to the ballet angel to do her stuff, and left Brenda to do what she wanted. She went to school and to her dancing lessons in perfect control, and kept her face still. Nobody but me realised that she was in more pain every day. I felt sick with worry.

For the Charity Show, Brenda told Mum she couldn't go backstage to help with the costumes and make-up, as she had done for the Christmas one. "Great!" Mum said. "This time I'll have the chance to see the show!" It wasn't quite true, of course. She wanted to be in there, dressing her daughter for her big night, and I knew that if Brenda had asked, Mum would have been allowed in. But keeping her secret was more important to Brenda than anything, and it would let Mum see the show, as she said. And I had a feeling that was important. So I didn't say anything.

So Mum and I – Dad was working that night – got seats in the Gods, the upper circle, the highest seats in the theatre. That was all we could afford. "Never mind – there'll be plenty more nights," Mum giggled, high as a kite with happiness. "We'll save up and go into the front stalls when she does her first star performance in *The Sleeping Beauty* or *The Nutcracker!*"

We arrived early, to give Brenda plenty of time to change and warm up. We bought a programme for two shillings and climbed the red-carpeted stairs that got narrower and narrower as they went up and side-stepped gingerly out across the steep cliff face of seats to our places.

"Don't fall! You'd go over the edge and right down into the posh seats. You haven't got a parachute! We're so high we won't be able to see the dancers at the back of the stage," Mum commented. "But it doesn't matter. We'll see Brenda when she's near the front."

We sat and read the programme. "There's her name, look – 'Hopkins Academy of Music and Dance – *Swan Lake*. Soloists – Alexandra McGann, Brenda Matheson, Anne Carter'. Brenda's first proper programme! I'll keep this for ever in her scrapbook!" Mum said, smoothing the programme proudly. Bright with joy, she pointed down towards the royal box, all crimson and cream and gold curly-wurlies. "That's where Princess Margaret will sit. Wonderful, isn't it?"

I nodded, but in fact I wished it were all over.

The princess was 20 minutes late. When she arrived, at last, everyone clapped, but only politely. Even Mum was annoyed. They clapped harder for the conductor as he came in. I didn't know why, he hadn't done anything yet, but I clapped too. We all stood up while the orchestra played *God Save the Queen*, and then sat down again. The lights dimmed, and everybody rustled a bit as they settled down. Then the theatre fell silent. The proper music started and the huge, deep red curtains with gold fringes rose slowly.

The show started with tap-dancing, then a duet of singers. Then, after them, a band, a Gaelic choir, songs and dances from a musical, then a little boy played a trumpet. Then, at last, the Hopkins School of Ballet.

Brenda was the second soloist. The first one had one of the fast, snappy dances, and got a good round of applause. When Brenda came on, though, she made the other girl look like a scarecrow on stilts. She danced perfectly. Her face calm and serene, she wafted across the stage like a feather in the breeze of the music, light and delicate.

The swelling of her ankle was almost hidden by the wide ballet shoe ribbons wrapped tight around it.

When she reached her final pose, still and pretty as a bone china statue, there was a moment of silence before the applause. "That's marvellous!" Mum shouted to me over all the noise – I couldn't have heard if she'd whispered. "Just that second of silence – that's better than clapping right away. It shows they've really been watching and enjoying it! Wait till you hear them when she comes out for her bow!"

Smiling, almost glowing with glory, Brenda curtsied deeply and skipped off with that smooth, toe-pointing ballerina glide. She didn't come back for a second bow, though the audience wanted her to.

Mum lost her beaming smile, and frowned as the third soloist came on, and, after her, the rest of the dancers.

Brenda didn't join the line-up for the whole school bow, either.

I was biting my lip. What had happened?

Mum looked at me, and at the row of smiling faces on the stage, and then stood up and shoved me out towards the end of the row, trampling on people's feet, rushing me along the tiny, cramped, dangerous ledge of seats as if it were a pavement. We hurried down the stairs and along the corridors, through the narrow door from the plush theatre entrance hall to the brick walls of the backstage area. The porter there tried to keep us out, but nothing could have stopped Mum at that minute.

We could hear the music for the next act. Miss Hopkins was standing by the stage door, white as a sheet. Some of the other girls were crying. A cut-off knot of white ribbon lay trampled in a corner.

Brenda was already being carried out to an ambulance.

Chapter 6
Brenda's Secret

Brenda had TB – tuberculosis – in the bones of that ankle. We found she'd gone to a doctor, not our own one who would have told Mum, but a stranger. She had given a false name and address and asked about her ankle. He said it could be cured, but she'd have to stop dancing for at least a year. Brenda would have missed the show, and the chance of being seen by the Sadler's

Wells man. That show was all she thought and dreamed about. So she'd kept it secret, danced elegantly on rotting bones, hiding her agony to win her moment of triumph. Then, just as she came off stage, the bones crumpled and crushed under the strain.

Mum never forgave me.

She was right, too. Yes, I was just a kid.

But if I'd done what I should have and told Mum ...

If I hadn't been scared and tried to cop out by leaving it all to Brenda ...

If I hadn't relied on a stupid angel statue ... .

A letter offering a free place at Sadler's Wells came the next week.

Brenda never danced again. She got a job at a dentist's.

I've never been cruel enough to ask her if it was worth it.

Barrington Stoke would like to thank all its readers for commenting on the manuscript before publication and in particular:

Dorcas Bakone
Anthea Beale
Chloe Beaton
Jolene Cheung
Sam Edmonds
Stevie-Jade Gatrell
Sue Gerrish
Marcelina Hamilton
Avni Jethwa
Sharon Lloyd
McKenzie Lloyd-Smith
Victoria Macadam
Jennifer Maidment

Katherine Moore
Ashley Murphy
Navita Pahuja
Stephanie Pears
Angharad Rees
Amanda Rennie
Leanne Richards
Julia Rizzo
Sarah Rizzo
Sue Rockell
Kate Tyler
Greta Walker
Ronald Yap

Become a Consultant!

Would you like to give us feedback on our titles before they are published? Contact us at the address below – we'd love to hear from you!

Barrington Stoke, Sandeman House, Trunk's Close,
55 High Street, Edinburgh EH1 1SR
Tel: 0131 557 2020 Fax: 0131 557 6060
E-mail: info@barringtonstoke.co.uk
Website: www.barringtonstoke.co.uk